The engines on the Island of Sodor love the summer. Sometimes The Fat Controller holds concerts.

One morning the engines were very excited. Alicia Botti, the famous singer, was coming to Sodor to sing at The Fat Controller's concert.

"I'm bound to be chosen
to collect her," boasted James.
"I'm the brightest and
the shiniest engine!"
"Nonsense!
I'm the most important!"
huffed Gordon.
Thomas wanted to feel
important, too.
"He might choose me,"
he said, hopefully.

Percy pulled up next to Gordon.

His face was very grimy.

"Well, one thing's for sure,"

snorted Gordon,

"He won't choose dirty Percy."

"I'm dirty because I work hard,"

said Percy proudly.

And he wheeshed away.

The next day The Fat Controller came
to decide which engine would collect
the singer from the Docks.
He didn't choose Gordon.
And he didn't
choose James.
He chose Thomas!
"Make sure Annie and
Clarabel are squeaky clean," he said.
"Yes, sir!" said Thomas proudly.
He felt very important indeed.

Thomas hurried off to be cleaned.

He parked next to Percy.

"Move aside," said Thomas.

"I'm the important engine today."

"But I need a washdown!" wailed Percy.

"My passengers will laugh at me."

"You'll have to wait," huffed Thomas.

"Today I have to be squeaky clean."

"Then I'll have to go without being

cleaned," said Percy, unhappily.

"I'm a guaranteed connection!"

He chuffed away, still very dirty.

Soon Thomas was shiny
and squeaky clean.
He felt more important than ever.
But as the workers coupled Annie
and Clarabel together,
they heard a strange noise.
A funny sort of squeak.

"What's that?"
asked Thomas, anxiously.
His Driver quickly oiled Annie
and Clarabel's undercarriage.
"That should take care of the
annoying squeak," he said.

On the way to the Docks,

Thomas heard the squeak again.

He was worried.

What could it be?

At the Docks, a big liner had

brought lots of passengers

to the Island of Sodor.

Alicia Botti was waiting

with The Fat Controller.

Thomas squeaked

into the quayside.

The Fat Controller held Clarabel's
door open for the famous singer.
He was pleased to see Thomas looking
so clean and shiny. But as Alicia Botti
was boarding the train, she saw
a mouse inside the carriage!
"SQUEAK!"
said the mouse.
"EEEEK! A mouse!"
screamed Alicia Botti.
And she screamed
and screamed and screamed.

She screamed so loud and so long that windows broke all over town. Alicia Botti was very cross indeed. "I can't possibly travel in coaches full of mice," she said.
The Fat Controller was very embarrassed. Thomas didn't feel important at all.

Just then, Percy returned from his guaranteed connection. He looked grimier than ever.

"Just look at the little green engine," Alicia Botti exclaimed.

"So sweet… and dirty! Like a proper steam engine!"

The Fat Controller called Percy over at once.

Alicia Botti boarded the train and Percy steamed away.

He felt very proud.

Later that day,
Thomas was waiting
at the washdown when
Percy chuffed up beside him.
"I'm sorry I was so cheeky,"
said Thomas.
"You go first."
"Thanks, Thomas. It's good to be
friends again," said Percy.
"But where is your mouse?"
"You'll see!" grinned Thomas.

The Fat Controller had made
the mouse her very own home
in the corner of Tidmouth sheds.
And Thomas named her
Alicia.

MAGIC Storytime Theatre

3 Fun Modes!

1
Listen And Watch
Projects storybook imagery, but lets you tell the story at your own pace.

2
Read Along
Tells the story automatically and turns off when the story is finished.

3
Bedtime Mode
Tells the story and displays storybook imagery. You control the action with the turn of a page.